WELCOME T͟he W͟orld

of
Geronimo Stilton

Published by Sweet Cherry Publishing Limited
Unit 36, Vulcan House,
Vulcan Road,
Leicester, LE5 3EF
United Kingdom

First published in the UK in 2020
2020 edition

2 4 6 8 10 9 7 5 3 1

ISBN: 978-1-78226-527-6

Text by Geronimo Stilton
Art Director: Iacopo Bruno
Graphic Designer: Laura Dal Maso / theWorldofDOT
Original cover illustration by Roberto Ronchi (design) and Mirka Andolfo, Studio Parlapà (colour)
Concept of illustration by Larry Keys, produced by Paolo De Capite and Daria Cerchi
Initial and final page illustrations by Roberto Ronchi and Ennio Bufi, MAD5 (design) and Studio
Parlapà and Andrea Cavallini (colour). Map illustrations by Andrea Da Rold and Andrea Cavallini
Cover layout and typography by Margot Reverdiau
Interior layout and typography by Claire Catlin
Graphics by Merenguita Gingermouse and Michela Battaglin
© 2000-2015 Edizioni Piemme S.p.A., Palazzo Mondadori – Via Mondadori, 1 – 20090 Segrate
© 2020 UK edition, Sweet Cherry Publishing
International Rights © Atlantyca S.p.A. – via Leopardi 8, 20123 Milano, Italy
Translation © 2006 by Atlantyca S.p.A.

Original title: *Un camper color formaggio*
Based on an original idea by Elisabetta Dami

www.geronimostilton.com/uk

www.sweetcherrypublishing.com

Printed and bound in Turkey
T.IO006

Geronimo Stilton

A CHEESE-COLOURED CAMPER VAN

Sweet Cherry

Mr. Stilton, Wait!

One morning, I was in a **FABUMOUSE** mood. I woke up before my alarm clock went off.

I made myself a delicious CHEESY good breakfast. And I got a seat on the Underground. Not an easy thing to do in crowded New Mouse City!

I was humming a **happy** tune when I reached my office.

Just then, my secretary came racing up to me. "**MR. STILTON**," she squeaked. "Don't open that door!"

But I had already turned the knob.

How strange. **Someone was sitting at my desk.**

GRANDFATHER WILLIAM SHORTPAWS

He was a **LARGE** mouse with silver fur and shiny steel glasses. He was holding my phone in one paw. The other paw flipped through my desk calendar. He looked so comfortable in my chair, you'd think he owned the place. And, well, he did.

You see, the mouse was my grandfather. Grandfather William Shortpaws. He was the founder of the company.

Oops. I completely forgot to introduce myself. My name is Stilton, *Geronimo Stilton*. I am a publisher. I run the most popular newspaper in New Mouse City. It's called The Rodent's Gazette.

But where was I? Oh, yes, I was staring at my grandfather. "**HELLO, GRANDFATHER**," I squeaked. "How are you?"

THREE, I SAID THREEEEE!

"HOW DO YOU THINK?" roared Grandfather William. "I'm busy! Very busy, that's how I am!"

I gulped. Can you believe I am afraid of my own grandfather? But I don't let it get to me. You see, everyone is afraid of Grandfather William. He is one tough, no-nonsense mouse. Once he made a five-kilo rat cry just by glaring at him.

Now he was **SCREAMING** into my phone. I felt sorry for the poor mouse on the other end.

"Yes, three!" he shrieked. "I need 3 million guidebooks to Ratzikistan on the double! I said, **THREE!** **THREE!** **THREEEE!**

10

T as in **Try harder!**
H as in **Hop to it!**
R as in **Right away!**
E as in **Exactly what I said!**
E as in **End of discussion!**"

He snickered. Then he **SLAMMED** down the phone.

I chewed my whiskers. "Um, what are you doing here, Grandfather?" I asked in a faint voice. "And why do you want to print three million guidebooks to **RATZIKISTAN?**"

As usual, Grandfather ignored me. He is the worst listener. Instead, he began scribbling away on my notepad.

Just then, my secretary, Mousella MacMouser, came in. She handed Grandfather a stack of papers. He leafed through them, grumbling.

"These are all wrong!" he snorted. "Wrong, wrong, wrong!" He tore up the papers and crumpled them into a ball. Then he jumped onto my desk. He struck a pose just like a professional basketball

mouse. "Score!" he squeaked, shooting the ball into my bin.

My secretary and I looked at each other in shock.

"The business is a mess, Geronimo!" he snorted. "You need to publish some **bestsellers** now or you can say bye-bye to your books forever!"

I had no idea what Grandfather was squeaking about. The company was doing great. The newspaper was selling like CHEESE ICE LOLLIES in the summertime. And our books always sold well. Yes, we hadn't had a bestseller in a few months, but we were still making tonnes of money.

Of course, Grandfather William wouldn't listen. "Don't tell **ME** how we're doing!" he shrieked. "I built this company with my bare paws! I know everything!"

Uh-oh. This was going to be a lot harder than I thought. Once Grandfather gets an idea in his head, it sticks like a mouse in a glue trap. He's like the safe at the Regal Rodent Bank. A tough one to crack.

I tried reasoning with him. "Um, but, Grandfather," I began in a gentle voice. "Twenty years ago, you left running the company to me. Isn't this my job?"

Can you guess his reply? Naturally, he didn't say a word. I told you my grandfather never listens.

He was staring at my calendar. "Look at all these appointments!" he squeaked. "I'm going to be busier than a **ratburglar** in the middle of a blackout."

"But, Grandfather!" I complained. "Those are my appointments!"

At that very moment, the phone **RANG**.

We both leaped for it. Unfortunately, the old mouse beat me to it.

RING!
RING!

"No, this is not **GERONIMO STILTON**," he thundered. "I am his grandfather. And from today on, I am the one in charge. The head honcho. The boss. **THE BIG CHEESE.** Got it?" He slammed down the phone.

I was horrified. What would my clients think? Maybe Grandfather was right. The business was a mess. **And it was all because of him!**

THE BIG CHEESE

15

NOT EVEN
PENGUINS ...

Right then, I remembered about the guidebooks. "Grandfather, can you at least tell me about these guidebooks to **RATZIKISTAN?**" I asked. "I just don't understand."

Grandfather William shook his head. "Poor Geronimo," he scoffed. "Of course you don't understand. Can you help it if your brain is so small? So teeny-weeny? So microscopic? Not everyone can be a genius like me."

By now, I was ready to strangle him. But how could I? I could just see the headlines in the paper the next day:

YOUNG PUBLISHER MURDERS FEEBLE OLD GRANDFATHER! STILTON SNUFFS OUT INNOCENT LIFE!

No, I couldn't do it. After all, I'm a newspaper mouse. I hate bad press.

Instead, I tried again. "Are you really going to print three million copies?" I asked.

For once, Grandfather William seemed to hear me. He rolled his eyes. "Wake up, **GERONIMO!** Wake up! WAKE UUUUUUP!" he shouted in my ear. Then he waved a map under my snout.

"What's that?" I mumbled, taken by surprise. He sneered and shoved the map at me again. This time I could see it clearly. It was a map of **RATZIKISTAN.**

"Have you ever noticed that there are no guidebooks to Ratzikistan?" Grandfather demanded.

I opened my mouth to reply, but he was already babbling on.

"Ah, Ratzikistan," Grandfather said with a sigh. "A place no one has ever heard of before. Just think of all of the **guidebooks** we can sell!" He clapped his paws. "Sometimes I am so smart, I scare myself!" he chuckled.

I was stunned. Had Grandfather William's cheese finally slipped off his cracker? No one goes to Ratzikistan. **NOT EVEN PENGUINS**.

"But Grandfather," I began. "There are no guidebooks to Ratzikistan because the temperature there is **forty degrees below zero!**"

MY SWEET LITTLE CHEESE CURL!

Suddenly, the office door flew open. In marched my sister, Thea. She is The Rodent's Gazette's special correspondent. Have you met her? You would remember Thea. She's one of a kind. Kind of a **NUT**, that is.

"Grandpa, dear Grandpa!" my sister squeaked. She threw herself into Grandfather's open paws.

Immediately, his eyes filled with tears.

"Thea, my beloved granddaughter! **My sweet little cheese curl!** More precious than my wallet! More beautiful than Miss Mouse Island!" he cried.

Thea smiled sweetly. "See your sister, here, Geronimo?" my grandfather added proudly. "Now, this is one smart rodent!"

Can you tell that Thea is Grandfather William's **favourite?** He sends her on all of these wonderful assignments. In fact, she had just returned from a trip to the **Southern Islands**. She was researching the latest trends in swimwear. *Tough job, I'm sure.*

"Well, it seems this year it's all about colour!" Thea announced. "Orange, red, yellow, green! You name it, they're wearing it!"

Grandfather beamed. "**BRILLIANT!** I'm so proud of you, darling!" he gushed.

I tried not to act jealous. But I was. I cleared my throat. "Um, I would love to go to the Southern Islands sometime, too," I offered timidly. Grandfather William shot me a disapproving look. "Forget it," he squeaked. "Only a **stunning** mouse like Thea can report on fashion. She's got style. Too bad I can't say the same about you."

I chewed my whiskers to keep from squeaking. What was wrong with the way I dressed? OK, so maybe I was a little on the conservative side. I wasn't into **flashy** colours or CRAZY prints. But no one had ever picked on my clothes before.

Grandfather turned to Thea. "How was the flight, **darling**?" he asked. "I hope your first-class seat was comfortable. Nothing but the best for my little treasure."

Did I mention Thea is Grandfather's favourite?

21

TINA SPICYTAIL

Right then, the phone rang. I pressed the speaker button so we could all listen.

"HEEEEELLO! HEEEEEELLOOOOO!" squeaked the female voice at the other end. I recognised it right away. It was Tina Spicytail, Grandfather's housekeeper.

"Mr. Geronimo, would you please ask Mr. Shortpaws what he would like for dinner?" she yelled. Tina was not a quiet mouse.

Grandfather William scratched his head. "Let's see, I'd like a CHEDDAR FONDUE ..." he began.

But Tina quickly interrupted him. "**NO FONDUE FOR YOU, MR. SHORTPAWS!**" she shrieked. "You're on a diet! By the way, are you wearing your woollen underwear? You're not so

22

young anymore, you know! Don't come crying to me if you catch a **terrible cold!**"

Grandfather rolled his eyes. He started to reply, but she cut him off again.

"Before I forget, I'm packing your suitcases for your trip," she announced. "I must have packed forty at least. I had a little trouble with your *antique desk*, though. But don't worry, I just chopped it up into **pieces**. You can put it together when you arrive at your destination."

Steam poured out of Grandfather William's ears. His eyes popped open wide.

"WHAT?!" he thundered. "Do you mean you chopped up my precious antique desk with the imported ivory knobs?" Uh-oh. I had a feeling Grandfather wasn't going to like the answer to that question.

"You got it!" Tina confirmed proudly. She went on to explain that she had also included his favourite armchair. It was chopped into pieces like the desk. "I am all ready to leave. I will be there in a couple of minutes!" she finished.

A dial tone filled the room. And an **ALARM BELL** went off inside my head. Grandfather was leaving? Where was he going? And why?

Just then, he turned to me. "Better get packing, Geronimo," he said. "You know how slow you are. You don't want to make us late."

I had no idea what he was talking about. *I* wasn't planning on going anywhere.

Grandfather William shook his head. "Oops, didn't we tell you?" he said.

Thea raised her eyebrows. "Oops, didn't we tell you?" she echoed.

Right then, my cousin Trap strode into the room. He was wearing a huge backpack. "Oops, didn't we tell you?" he squeaked.

The door flew open again. This time, Tina marched in. She was pushing an **enormouse** trunk on wheels. She looked at everyone staring at me.

"Didn't you tell him?" she shouted.

I bit my tail in a fit of rage. "Tell me what? **WHAT DIDN'T YOU TELL ME?**" I screamed.

At that moment, my favourite nephew, Benjamin, raced through the door and hugged me. "Uncle Geronimo! I am so happy!" he cried. **"They just told me that you are coming with us to Ratzikistan!"**

25

Ratzikistan, Here We Come!

I was flabbergasted. "We are leaving for **RATZIKISTAN?** Why didn't anyone tell me?" I shouted.

No one squeaked. What could they say? They knew they were wrong.

Instead, Thea shoved a chocolate **Cheesy Chew** into my mouth. "Don't get your tail in a twist," she soothed in a honey-sweet voice.

I was still **fuming**. But I must admit, I do love those **Cheesy Chews**. There's nothing like a yummy piece of chocolate to perk me up. Still, I wasn't giving in so easily. I was tired of being overlooked. "I will not be ignored!" I spluttered with my mouth full.

Trap rolled his eyes. "You're such a drama queen, **GERMEISTER**," he chuckled. He glanced at his watch. "Better shake a paw, Cuz. You have exactly seventeen and a half minutes to pull yourself together, pack your suitcases, and put on the alarm system before we're off!" he added. Then he pinched my cheek, causing the **Cheesy Chew** to go down the wrong pipe.

"ARGH! ARGH!" I gagged.

Grandfather clapped a paw on my back. The chocolate flew across the room.

"My dear grandson, quit complaining. We'd never ignore you!" he insisted. "Now stop dilly-dallying and close your suitcases."

I gnashed my teeth together. I took a deep breath. Then I explained in a very small voice why I couldn't close my suitcases. **I didn't have any!**

"Even better!" Grandfather William concluded. "Then you can leave without them! Let's go! Call a taxi!"

By now, I was beyond mad. I was a **raging** ball of fur. I dug my paws into the carpet.

"I'm not leaving! And you can't make me!" I squeaked.

Yes, I sounded just like a five-year-old mouslet. But I didn't care.

Grandfather William stared at me for a moment. Then he told everyone to leave the room.

"I need to be alone with my dear grandson!" he exclaimed.

As soon as they left, Grandfather **slumped** against me. Then he limped over to my chair. *Since when did he have a limp?* I wondered.

28

"Ah, Grandson, getting old is such a horrible thing. You are so lucky to be young and strong," he said in a feeble voice.

I blinked. I had never thought about Grandfather William being old before. He was so loud. And tough. And, well, **obnoxious**.

"Are you OK, Grandfather?" I asked, feeling guilty.

He shook his head. "I'm not feeling well. I have a pain right here, near my heart," he said, pointing at his breast pocket.

I raised my eyebrows. "But, Grandfather, that's your wallet," I pointed out.

He shrugged. "Ah, yes. My heart, my wallet, same thing," he added.

I wasn't surprised. Grandfather loves money more than **CHEESE**. He's the cheapest mouse I know. He once shaved off all of his fur to save money on shampoo and conditioner. That's why they call him **CHEAP MOUSE WILLY**.

Now he stroked his fur, looking sad. "It kills me to see our family arguing," he mumbled. "I am so hurt that you don't want to come with us."

He sighed. Then his eyes filled with tears.

I didn't know what to say. I didn't want to leave. But I had never seen Grandfather so broken up.

"Say you are coming with us, dear grandson!" he cried, grabbing my paw. "Please say yes! Do it for me. I have given you **SO MUCH** and I ask for so little."

By now, he was sobbing away full force. I had never seen so many tears come out of one rodent before. He would have come in handy when my Aunt Sweetfur's mouse hole went up in FLAMES.

At last, I couldn't stand his sobs any longer. "OK, OK. I'll come," I muttered.

At that very moment, the unthinkable happened. Grandfather William leaped back to his feet. It was a miracle! It was as if he were suddenly thirty years younger.

"Well, then, let's hit the road!" he shrieked. "The taxi is here!"

He flung open the office door. Thea, Trap, and Benjamin fell on top of one another. Their ears had been pressed to the door.

"Wait, Grandfather!" I called. But he was already halfway down the hall.

"Move your tail, you spineless fool!" he shouted back at me.

GRANDFATHER'S SUPER CAMPER VAN

I COULDN'T BELIEVE IT. My own grandfather had set me up. I thought he really was sick. Even worse, I thought he was heartsick. Now I knew he was just nuts. Nuts enough to pull a low-down prank on me.

ROTTEN RATS' BREATH! I was in a sour mood. Anyone who knows me knows that I **HATE** travelling!

My grandfather, on the other hand, was bursting with excitement.

"Isn't travelling great?" he squeaked happily. "In my next life, I think I will be an explorer. I will soar above the clouds in my own private jet. Sail the high seas in my yacht. And, of course, I will hit the road in my fabumouse **CHEESE-COLOURED CAMPER VAN**."

I sighed. Grandfather wasn't dreaming about the camper van. He really does have a cheese-coloured camper van. He ambles along in the fast lane at twenty miles per hour, annoying all of the other drivers. They flash their headlights at him. They **HONK** their horns. But there's no budging Grandfather. He's like a snail on a motorway.

Actually, Grandfather doesn't drive a camper van. He drives a **SUPER-CAMPER VAN**. It's longer than fifty mice standing tail to tail.

It's painted a deep cheddar yellow. And it's filled with everything you can imagine.

The driver's cabin has a `satellite navigation system`. It lets you pinpoint your position anywhere around the world.

Kitchen

Dining Room

Bathroom

An enormous **crystal chandelier** hangs in the camper van's dining room. This is where Grandfather William likes to eat Tina's five-course gourmet meals. Grandfather's bedroom has a four-poster bed and its own marble bathroom. There's even a yellow Jacuzzi **SHAPED LIKE A SLICE OF CHEESE!**

Besides all of that, there are a couple of guest rooms, an elegant library filled with old books, and

Bedroom **Grandfather's Office**

a room just for luggage. The place is bigger than my entire mouse hole!

Oh, and I didn't even tell you about the kitchen. It's a cook's **dream**. It has a real stone oven. And a computerised giant refrigerator. It tells you when supplies are getting low. Tina loves it. Of course, she travels with Grandfather wherever he goes. Yep, Tina and her extendable rolling pin. She never leaves home without it. It was a gift from Grandfather. At night, she keeps the rolling pin within paw's reach for protection. Once she accidentally knocked Grandfather William over the head with it. She thought he was a **ratburglar!**

Still, Tina does a lot more than just cook. In fact, she's one multi-talented rodent. She can give an injection and fix a flat tyre without twitching a whisker. And even more important, Tina keeps Grandfather in line. She's the only rodent I know who is not afraid of him. **As I said, she's one tough mouse!**

KING OF THE ROAD

At last, we were ready to leave. Grandfather drove down the block. Two minutes later, we discovered we had a little problem. No, make that two little problems. Benjamin and Trap had come down with **RODENT POX!** They were covered from head to paw with red bumps. We returned home to drop them off.

Now there were only four of us. Grandfather, of course, sat behind the wheel. Tina **BANGED** pots and pans in the kitchen. My sister took pictures, leaning out the window. And I read the map. I tried to give Grandfather William directions, but as usual, he wouldn't listen. When I told him to turn left, he insisted on turning right.

"Don't be a back-seat driver, Grandson!" he barked. "I know where we're going. You forget, I've travelled all over the world. I have my own map right here inside the old noggin." He tapped his head. "Yep, I've got a memory like a steel trap. I can find my way to the Swiss Cheese Islands with my eyes closed. I can make it to Mouse Everest with one paw tied behind my back. I can even walk and chew cheese at the same time."

In the end, we got **LOST.**

We travelled for hours along a deserted road.

THE RIGHT WAY TO RATZIKISTAN

We didn't pass one single road sign.

By nightfall, we found ourselves in the middle of a forest. Grandfather didn't seem to mind. He just kept driving and driving.

I tried to use the super-high-tech **satellite navigation system**. But it was so confusing. And the instruction manual was missing.

Finally, Grandfather pulled over. "I think I'll take a rest," he announced. "Who wants to drive?"

No one squeaked. Do you want to know why? It's an absolute nightmare driving with Grandfather. He barks out orders the whole time. He even throws a fit if you blink! Grandfather William says he is **KING OF THE ROAD**.

Sometimes he even wears a crown while he's driving. It was a joke gift from Trap. But Grandfather took it seriously.

"Who's taking the wheel? No time for dilly-dallying!" Grandfather shouted now. **"I can't do it all! Even a genius needs to rest sometimes."**

GERONIMO, DO SOMETHING!

We were all in a panic. We couldn't keep driving. We were terribly lost.

"Geronimo, do something!" Thea whispered to me. "Maybe you can go out and look for help."

I turned pale. Me? Go out into the deep, dark woods? I'd rather cut off my tail. Well, OK, maybe not my tail. Maybe my whiskers. Or maybe just some fur.

"Wh-wh-why m-m-m-me?" I stammered.

My sister gave me a look. "Oh, stop being such a scaredy-mouse, **Geronimoid**," she scolded. "I'd go myself but I haven't showered. What if I ran into a cute mouse?"

I rolled my eyes. My sister goes on more dates than Sylvia Sizzlefur, the famouse movie star.

Just then, Tina winked at my sister. She waved her rolling pin at me. "Mr. Stilton, would you mind going outside for a minute to see if it is raining?" she asked.

I had barely left the cabin when ... **SLAM!**

The door shut behind me. I heard the lock click.

CHEESE NIBLETS! I had been tricked again! I screamed for them to let me in, but no one answered.

I was all alone.

In the dark, spooky woods!

I heard my sister singing in the shower. She'd probably be in there for an hour – and then spend another hour fluffing her fur! It was as if she'd forgotten about me! Didn't she care about me at all?

Tina was back in the kitchen. I could hear her rolling pin slamming the countertop.

What was she making this time? A double-cheese lasagne? **A CHEDDAR CASSEROLE?**

I sobbed. I would never get a chance to find out. I just knew something horrible was going to happen. I mean, I was in the middle of the wilderness. And it was so dark.

What if a wild animal attacked me? What if I fell off an icy cliff?

What if space mice picked me up and brought me back to their leader?

Oh, how could my sister do this to me? She's the one who's not afraid of anything. She is the bravest mouse I know. **Nothing scares her!**

She loves:

1. PARACHUTING OFF DANGEROUS MOUNTAINTOPS

2. RACING HER MOTORCYCLE

3. PRACTICING KARATE (SHE'S A BLACK BELT)

4. DOING STUNTS WITH HER AEROPLANE

5. EXTREME SURVIVAL CAMPS

Yes, my sister, Thea, is one courageous mouse. She's not afraid of anything or anyone.

I looked around, shivering. The forest was as black as ink. Luckily, I remembered I had a tiny torch attached to my keyring. I pulled it out. The light was faint.

Are you afraid of the dark? **I AM!**

Shadows loomed everywhere. The branches on the trees looked like skeletons reaching for the sky. Moths transformed into bats. A bird screeched overhead. **I gulped.** My paws shook so hard, I almost dropped the torch.

Then I saw a shadow. It was behind me.

It was big. It was furry. It had a long tail.

"RAT-MUNCHING RATTLESNAKES!"

I screeched. "Who are you? What do you want?!"

No one answered. So I ran like crazy.

The shadow followed. I tripped. The shadow tripped, too. I got up. The shadow got up, too.

Just then, it hit me. I was running from my own shadow!

STILTON HIMSELF?

I stopped. I wanted to go back to the camper van. But now I had no idea where I was. I started running down a path. It had to lead somewhere, right?

I ran and ran and ran ... until I tripped again. Did I mention I'm a bit of a klutz? My snout banged into the ground. **OUCH!**

I sat up in a daze. That's when I saw him. A furry rodent staring down at me.

"Grandfather?" I mumbled. "How did you find me? Where's the camper van?"

The other rodent flashed a blinding light in my eyes. "Grandfather?" he repeated. He sounded confused.

I stood up. No, this wasn't my cranky Grandfather. It was a stranger. He had a big square head, a square snout, and square shoulders. Even his tail looked square. How odd.

"Who are you? What do you want?" he squeaked warily.

I told him my whole tale. About Grandfather William, the super camper van, and getting lost. I left out the part about me running from my shadow. I didn't want him to make fun of me. After all, we had just met.

Then I told him my name, **GERONIMO STILTON.**

"Stilton!" he exclaimed. "Geronimo Stilton, the famouse writer? I have read all of your books!" He shook my paw, excitedly. "My name is Sylvester Squaretail," he announced. "May I have your autograph? With my name, too?"

I grinned. I must admit I love running into my fans. They're so **sweet**. So **sincere**. So **smart**. How do I know they're smart? They must be. They like to read my books!

I didn't have any paper, so I wrote my autograph on a leaf. I hoped Sylvester didn't drop it in the woods. He'd never find it in this **DARK**, **CREEPY** place.

DOUBLE-CHEESE LASAGNE

Sylvester slipped the leaf into his pocket. I could tell he was one happy rodent.

I chewed my whiskers. I'd be happy, too, if I could find my way back to the camper van. And what about Ratzikistan? Maybe Sylvester knew how to get there.

"RATZIKISTAN!" he exclaimed when I asked. "You're in the middle of the Fossil Forest. Ratzikistan is in the opposite direction."

CHEESE NIBLETS! I knew Grandfather had been driving the wrong way. I groaned.

"Don't worry," said Sylvester. "I can tell you how to get back to your camper van. Then I'll give you directions to **RATZIKISTAN**."

It took him half an hour to explain everything. There was a lot to remember. I thought about writing everything down on some leaves. But I didn't want to rip up ten bushes. I love nature too much.

Sylvester shook my paw and said goodbye. "Have a safe trip!" he called, heading off.

I started down the path. As I walked, I mumbled the directions.

"Let's see, I take the path for ten minutes until I reach the beech tree," I began. "Or was it an **OAK TREE?** Then I turn right two or three times and cross the brook. At the brook, I head upstream, or maybe downstream. Then I come to a boulder shaped like a cat's head. Or was it a rat's head? Then I cross a small bridge and turn left, then right. No, maybe it was right, then left …"

I tramped through the woods for more than an hour. *RATS!* I was lost again. Oh, why didn't I write those directions down? So what if I destroyed a few bushes? So what if there were fewer leaves in the world? Was that such a crime?

I sat down on a rock. Tears sprang to my eyes. "How did I get myself into such a mess?" I sobbed. "It's late and I'm hungry. I should be home in my cosy mouse hole. I should be nibbling on a triple-decker cheese-and-tomato toastie right now."

Just then, I sniffed the air. Was I dreaming? Did I really smell **CHEESE?**

I sniffed again. Yes, I was sure of it. It was the scent of a **DOUBLE-CHEESE LASAGNE!** I pulled myself together and got back on the path. I followed the heavenly scent. Before long, I spotted the twinkling lights of the camper van.

I squeaked with joy. Home at last!

I couldn't wait to tell my family about my adventures. They would be so happy to see me. They must have been worried sick when I didn't return. Inside, I found them all seated at the table.

Thea glanced up. "Oh, it's just **GERONIMO**."

"Who?" asked Grandfather.

"GERONIMO!" Thea repeated.

Grandfather William shoved more lasagne into

Double-cheese lasagne

his mouth. "Oh, did he go out?" he muttered.

I sank onto the sofa. I told them how I got lost. Then I explained about the lasagne. "I followed the scent back to the camper van," I said.

Tina smiled. She was very proud of her cooking. Especially her **DOUBLE-CHEEJE LAJAGNE**.

"Speaking of lasagne," I continued. "Can you cut me a piece?"

Now Tina was practically glowing. "Nope, it's all gone!" she announced triumphantly. She held up the empty pan. "Your grandfather even licked the pan clean. So much for his diet," she added.

My **STOMACH RUMBLED** in protest. I couldn't believe my family hadn't saved a single piece of Tina's delicious lasagne for me! I was starving after my midnight ramble through the forest.

Oh, why had I come on this miserable trip?

FIVE POUNDS OF CHEDDAR

The next day, we left at dawn. I pointed Grandfather in the right direction.

For once, he listened to me. What a shock. Maybe he was feeling sick. I didn't ask. I was just happy to be moving again.

"Oh, I'm a travelling mouse! Whoa! Whoa! Whoa! I'm a travelling mouse!" Grandfather William sang.

I groaned. Grandfather's singing sounded like the shrieks of a mouse with his tail caught in a trap.

We drove farther and farther north. The landscape began to change. Instead of green trees and bushes, there were snow-covered valleys. Icy mountains dotted the horizon. I noticed that the sunlight was getting dimmer and dimmer. It seemed we had left autumn behind and headed straight into winter. And it wasn't just any old winter. It was the **COLDEST** winter on the planet.

At lunch, we stopped for a break. I put on my thermal underwear. I put on my heavy parka. I put on my cat-fur hood. But nothing kept the cold out. The air froze my whiskers. I had to defrost them back in the camper van.

We drove on and on. Weeks went by. Finally, one day, a road sign emerged through the fog.

R-A-T-Z-I-K-I-S-T-A-N

"**RATZIKISTAN!** Cheese niblets, I did it! We're here!" Grandfather William exclaimed. He pulled over.

"I must find a supermarket immediately," Tina declared.

I stared out into the fog. "Something tells me there aren't any supermarkets in **RATZIKISTAN**," I told her. "In case you haven't noticed, we're in the middle of nowhere!"

Tina **snorted**. She grabbed her canvas shopping bag (no paper bags for Tina). Then she jumped out of the camper van. She looked around. Then she began hiking towards a dirty little store on the corner.

Rotting fruit and piles of smelly fish filled the store window. Inside, there were crates and boxes everywhere. What a dump. I peered into one of the crates. It was filled with jam jars. I picked one up. Little white balls of something floated in a murky liquid. They looked just like **EYEBALLS**. I gulped.

An army of ants crawled out the side of another box. Each ant carried a piece of **SMELLY GREEN CHEESE**. My stomach lurched.

Ears of shrivelled corn on the cob stuck out of a

wicker basket. I pulled one out and shrieked. It was covered with tiny WORMS.

By now, I was feeling faint. Did I tell you I'm afraid of ants? Did I tell you I'm afraid of worms? Did I tell you I'm not too crazy about electric toothbrushes, either? Oh, but that's another story ...

I watched as Tina marched up to the rodent behind the counter. He had a crooked tail and a crooked smile.

She pulled out a long shopping list. "I'll need five pounds of your best cheddar! Six tins of your finest sardines! **And three loaves of your freshest seven-grain bread!**" she barked.

The rodent dropped his crooked smile. His eyes opened wide. Still, he didn't say a word. After all, what could he say? It was clear they didn't have those things in this store. "Forget it, Tina," I whispered. "I told you this is not a regular supermarket. There are no supermarkets in **RATZIKISTAN**."

Tina stamped her paw. One thing you should know about Grandfather's housekeeper. She never takes no for an answer. And I mean **NEVER**. Once a waiter told Tina that she could not meet the chef at her favourite Italian restaurant, Squeakolini's. **She threw a fit**. First she threw her napkin in the air. Then she threw her spaghetti in the air. Then she threw her waiter in the air.

"I will not forget it," Tina insisted. She slapped her shopping list on the counter. "Give this to your boss," she told Crooked Tail.

He disappeared into the back of the store. A few minutes later, another rodent came out. He was carrying all the things Tina had asked for.

Tina shot me a smug look. **"No supermarkets, my paw!" she smirked.**

A CAST-IRON
STOMACH

We climbed back into the camper van. Tina put away the food. Soon Grandfather revved up the engine and we were off again.

I stared out the window as we drove along. Icy streams flowed down from the tops of gigantic glaciers. **SNOW-CAPPED** mountains dotted the landscape.

Thea snapped away with her camera. "This place is like a winter wonderland," she remarked.

We drove on into the night. The road grew steeper. We crossed over a narrow bridge. We climbed along a rugged gorge.

Patches of ice covered the road. I broke out in a cold sweat. One slip and we'd all be goners. We'd be

65

nothing but a camper van full of cat food. I felt faint. Oh, why had I come to **RATZIKISTAN**? It was one big mountain mess. And I was afraid of heights!

At last, we reached a clearing. It overlooked all of the valleys below.

Grandfather pulled over. He jumped out of the camper van, clapping his paws. "Now, this is what I call good clean air!" he squeaked, taking a deep breath. "Someone write this down. We need to tell tourists to stop at this very spot. The view is more breathtaking than the inside of the **Cheesy Chews** factory!"

My sister began typing away on her laptop. She had been taking notes the whole trip to put in our guidebook to **RATZIKISTAN**.

"What would I do without my **darling** granddaughter?" Grandfather William beamed. Then he scowled in my direction.

"It's a shame you're not more like your sister,

GERONIMO," he added. "It's a wonder you two are related!"

I decided to take a walk. My tail was flat from sitting in the camper van for so long. Plus, I needed to stretch my paws a little. Get the old **BLOOD** pumping. Get away from Grandfather.

I took a few steps, but I didn't get far. Seconds later, Tina's whistle practically pierced my eardrums. She uses it to signal that dinner is ready.

"Come on, shake a paw!" she called. **"You don't want your food to get cold!"**

We sat down at the table. Tina was busy dishing up the meal. She placed one olive and a piece of lettuce on Grandfather William's plate. Recently, she had decided he needed to go back on his diet.

Grandfather stared at his plate and sighed.

"**No complaining**," Tina scolded. "You need to drop those pounds or we'll have to roll you home!"

Then she turned her attention to me. **UH-OH**. Tina had other plans for me. Recently, she had decided that I was too thin. She began piling my plate high with food. I watched in horror as she filled an **ENORMOUSE** bowl to the brim with spaghetti. Then she slapped down plate after plate of pies, casseroles, puddings, bread, and more. There was no way I could eat all of that food. It was enough for ten mice, not one!

I felt sick. "Um, but, Tina," I began. "I have a weak stomach. I don't think—"

"**NONSENSE!**" Tina interrupted me. "I'll fix that stomach of yours. You just need to fill it with a ton of food. Soon you'll be able to eat stones!"

I cringed. But I didn't tell Tina I wasn't interested in eating stones. I didn't want her to hit the roof.

Meanwhile, Grandfather was eyeing my food with envy. He tried to steal a roll, but Tina slapped his paw away.

"I'm doing this for your own good!" she told Grandfather. "As for you, **GERONIMO**, you need to try harder!"

I opened my mouth to complain. Bad idea. Tina picked up a spoon and stuffed my mouth full of lard.

"See, that wasn't so bad, was it?" she chuckled.

I couldn't answer. Have you ever tasted lard? **Think glue, only ten times worse!**

TINA SPICYTAIL

THE SUN HAS BEEN KIDNAPPED!

That night, I had **HORRIBLE** dreams. First I was drowning in a vat of creamy butter and lard. Then I was being chased by a ten-foot ham-and-cheese sandwich waving a pickle.

I woke up with a **START**.

I stared out of my window. It was dark.

Was it still the middle of the night? No, my alarm clock said it was ten in the morning.

My fur stood on end. I woke up my sister.

"Thea! The sun has been kidnapped!" I squeaked.

NOT ME!

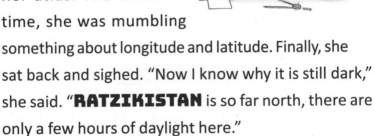

My sister looked at the picked up her globe. She punched in some numbers on her calculator. She pawed through her atlas. The whole time, she was mumbling something about longitude and latitude. Finally, she sat back and sighed. "Now I know why it is still dark," she said. "**RATZIKISTAN** is so far north, there are only a few hours of daylight here."

We started driving again.

The dark sky made me depressed. Who would buy a guidebook on a place where the sun never shines?

Oh, why did I come on this **miserable** trip? I could be at home warming my fur in the bright sunshine. I could be sipping a mozzarella milkshake at Happypaw's Outdoor Cafe. I could be planting yellow flowers in my garden. Well, OK, I didn't actually have a garden. But I always wanted one.

I was still **dreaming** about home when I realised something was wrong. We weren't moving. What was Grandfather doing? Stopping for another scenic view? It would be hard to see much in the dark.

'Well, that's it," Grandfather William announced. "We're out of petrol."

He took out a big can from under his seat.

Then he waved it under my snout.

"**SOMEONE** needs to find a petrol station," he squeaked, staring right at me.

I chewed my whiskers.

"Who's going to go?" I asked suspiciously. "Not me, I'm too old," **grumbled** Grandfather.

"Not me, I'm a lady," **squeaked** Thea.

"**Not me, I'm cooking!**" shouted Tina. "I'm making pizza."

I stared out the window. There was no way I was going out there. It was dark. The ground was frozen. There were no trees or bushes or happy woodland animals. We were miles away from civilisation. Not my kind of place. I like lots of rodents. I like taxis. I like bright lights. **Oh, how I missed New Mouse City!**

Two seconds later, Grandfather pushed me out the door.

Why does he never listen to me?

"Don't worry, **MR. GERONIMO!**" Tina called after me. "I'll keep a nice slice of pizza for you!"

I left the camper van. I had no choice. **They had locked the door behind me!**

COULD IT BE SANTA MOUSE?

Right then, I heard the sound of jingling bells. A mouse was coming towards me. He was riding a sledge pulled by reindeer.

I blinked. What was Santa Mouse doing in **RATZIKISTAN**? Christmas was already over.

I took a closer look. No, it wasn't Santa. It was just a local rodent on a sledge.

"Slow down, please!" I shouted. "I need a ride!"

But he didn't seem to understand. I waved my petrol can in the air. "I need petrol!" I tried.

He just smiled and zipped right by me.

I began running after him. My heart was pounding. My muscles ached. Sweat poured down my fur. If only I spoke Ratzikistani. Oh, **where was a good translator when you needed one**?

Suddenly, I spotted something up ahead. Could it be? Yes, it was. A little bus stop stood on a hill.

I gathered all of my strength and sprinted for it.

CHEESECAKE! Somehow I got there before the sledge. I held up my paw for him to stop.

This time he got it. "Stop?" he asked.

I nodded. I was so exhausted, I couldn't even squeak.

I pulled myself onto the sledge.

We took off at breakneck speed.

CRAZY RIDER

CHEESE NIBLETS! Sledge Mouse was a crazy driver. He was going so fast, it felt like we were flying. I held on for dear life. We **plunged** down steep slopes. We **rocketed** over lakes. I squeezed my eyes shut. Oh, when would this miserable ride be over?

Sledge Mouse didn't seem to notice I was shaking like a leaf. He kept chattering away. Of course, I had no idea what he was saying. Maybe it was better that way. I might have been even more **TERRIFIED**. I wasn't sure this rodent had all his marbles. He kept doing wacky things like dropping the reins to blow his nose. Or scratch his whiskers. Or eat a breath mint.

Each time the sledge went into a slide, I began to squeak. "Watch the road, I mean the snow, I mean **be careful!**" I cried.

Each time, he would burst out laughing. Did I say something funny? I wasn't trying to be funny. I was just trying to stay alive!

Why, oh, why had I climbed onto this sledge? I could have walked. I had two paws. So it might have taken me a little longer to get somewhere. So what? At least I wouldn't end up flattened in a sledge crash. I could just see the headlines now: **STILTON SQUISHED TO SMITHEREENS IN SLEDGE ACCIDENT! PUBLISHER SLIDES OFF THE FACE OF THE EARTH!**

I shivered. What a way to go. What a nightmare. What a strange glowing light in the distance! Could it be a petrol station? I blinked back tears. **HOLEY CHEESE!** It was! I stopped myself from breaking into a song and dance. I didn't want to set off the madmouse at the reins.

He screeched to a stop in front of the pump. I popped out of the sledge as fast as my quivering paws could take me. *"Thank you!"* I squeaked.

Sledge Mouse grinned. Then he took off. I must say, I wasn't entirely sad to see him go.

But now I had a new problem. How would I get back to the camper van? I filled up my can with petrol and paid the attendant.

The attendant introduced me to a mouse who was filling up his snowmobile. He offered me a ride. Before getting on, I asked him a few questions. *"You're a safe driver, right?"* I said. *"You don't go fast, right?"*

He laughed as if to say, "I'm the safest driver on the planet." Then he said something in Ratzikistani and gave me a crash helmet.

UH-OH. I wasn't feeling good about this. But what choice did I have? I had to get back to the camper van. Oh, why had I left it in the first place?

With a sigh, I climbed onto the snowmobile. **We took off like a pair of schoolmice on the first day of the summer holidays.**

Heeelp! How Do You Ride This Thing?

I couldn't believe it. It was happening all over again. I was off on another wild ride. Were all Ratzikistanis this crazy? I wondered. Or did I just get lucky? **RANCID RAT HAIRS!** It couldn't get any worse than this.

Could it?

Half an hour later, it did. The CRAZY MOUSE DRIVER started squeaking at me in Ratzikistani. For some reason, he kept pointing to the handlebars. What was he trying to tell me? I didn't have a clue. Maybe he was just showing me the parts of the snowmobile. I decided to play along. "Yes, the handlebars are for steering." I nodded. What next? The wheels? The horn? Did snowmobiles even have horns? I didn't know. I had never been on one before.

Just then, the driver tapped me on the back. He pointed to the handlebars again. Then he **FELL SOUND ASLEEP**. I tried waking him up. But it was no use.

"Help!" I shrieked in a panic. "How do you drive this thing?"

My cry rang out in the darkness. Of course, no one answered. What nutty rodent would be outside on such a freezing cold night? Or was it day? Who knew? It seemed like it was always night-time in **RATZIKISTAN**. Oh, how I hated this horrible, dark place.

Suddenly, I realised we were racing down an incredibly steep hill. "No!" I screamed. "I want to get off! I want to go home! I want my mummy!"

Next to me, I could hear my driver happily snoring away. Then the snowmobile hit the ground. It was a miracle. We were all still in one piece.

Finally, my driver woke up. He stretched. He yawned. Was this mouse for real? Couldn't he see we were speeding along out of control? Couldn't he see I was about to have a nervous breakdown?

Right then, a big **cheese-coloured** shape appeared before my eyes. It was the camper van!

Flashes of light snapped in the darkness. My sister, Thea, was taking pictures. **RATS!** My fur must look like a mess. But there was no time to worry about it now. "Where are the brakes?!" I shrieked in a panic.

At last, the driver took over. He spun around right in front of the camper van. I was thrown out of the snowmobile. I landed snout-first in an **ENORMOUSE** snowbank.

The driver tossed me the petrol can. Then he sped off.

My sister took one last picture of me with a snout full of icicles. "These pictures are perfect for our book!"

she declared. "And I've got the perfect caption: Fun times in **RATZIKISTAN!**"

I didn't have the strength to reply.

I dragged myself to the camper van. Could it get any worse? I wondered. And then it did. As soon as I walked in, Tina stuffed a sizzling slice of pizza into my mouth. Have you ever burned your tongue on hot pizza? I howled in pain.

"See, Mr. Geronimo, I told you I'd keep your pizza warm," Tina said proudly.

Why, oh, why had I come on such a crazy adventure?

I'm Not a Sportsmouse

We spent the next few days roaming around **RATZIKISTAN**. We tried to interview the locals. But it was hard. After all, they didn't speak English. We couldn't understand one squeak.

Then my sister decided one of us should try all of the local sports. Guess who was the lucky mouse? That's right, yours truly.

Oh, why does my family like to torture me? They know **I'm not a sportsmouse.** I'm always the last rodent picked for a team. Still, there I was, joining in on a ...

A. SNOWBALL FIGHT (They thrashed me two seconds after I made my first snowball.)

B. CONTEST FOR THE BEST-BUILT SNOWMOUSE (I accidentally knocked the head off when I tried to put on whiskers.)

C. MOUNTAIN HIKE (They carried me back on a stretcher.)

D. SKATING RACE (I fell through a crack in the ice. When they pulled me out, I was **FROZEN SOLID**.)

E. STINKY FISH CONTEST (I lost. But I'm telling you, mine was the stinkiest.)

F. CLASS ON HOW TO BUILD AN IGLOO (My door was so small, I was trapped inside.)

HEAVENLY CHEDDARELLA!

We were all feeling depressed.

It was clear **RATZIKISTAN** wasn't exactly a great vacation spot. "Who would want a guidebook to this place?" my sister said with a sigh. I shrugged. What could I say? Who would want to visit a place that was **forty degrees below zero?** A place where the sun never shines? A place where all the fish are *stinky?*

Thea switched off her laptop computer. It was time to go home. For once, even Grandfather William agreed.

Before we left, I took a short walk. I headed towards a nearby village.

I passed a house. Through the window, I saw a Ratzikistani family having dinner.

They were munching on a very tasty-looking golden-yellow cheese.

Right then, one of the mice saw me at the window. She invited me in. I tried to say no, but she didn't understand. She pulled me inside. Immediately, I was hit with the most **AMAZING** scent. It was coming from the golden-yellow cheese. The mouse cut me a slice. This time, I didn't refuse. I took a nibble. Then two. Then three. **CHEESECAKE!** It was the best cheese I had ever tasted in my life! It was more delicious than the chunkiest cheddar. It was more tasty than the best blue cheese. I was in heaven. I had to find out the name of that cheese.

"What do you call this?" I asked the mouse who had invited me in. She grinned. Then she said,

"CHEDDARELLA."

I shook my head. Was she making fun of me? It sounded like she'd said "**CHEDDAR,**" but it didn't taste like any cheddar I'd ever eaten.

"No," I tried again. "The name. Can you please tell me the name of this cheese?"

"CHEDDARELLA," she repeated in a louder voice.

Now I didn't know if she meant cheddar or mozzarella. Oh, why do mice like to tease me? Do I look like a pushover?

"Please, madam," I insisted. "I don't have time for jokes. I just want to know the name of this cheese."

This time she pounded the table. She picked up the cheese and held it under my snout.

"CHEDDARELLA! CHEDDARELLA! C-H-E-D-D-A-R-E-L-L-A!"

she squeaked at the top of her lungs.

I slapped my forehead. Now I got it. It was called Cheddarella cheese. Who would have thought such a scrumptious cheese would have such a funny name?

I ran to tell the others.

Don't Look So Worried ...

Thea was the most excited about the golden-yellow cheese. "I have the most brilliant idea!" she squeaked. That night, I heard her typing away on her computer. What was my crazy sister up to now?

You just never knew with Thea. One time, she tried to get into the fashion business. She began designing her own clothes. She made me test out all of her samples. I was running around in **Skirts** for weeks. *Everyone* at the office made fun of me. Lucky for me, Thea came to her senses. She realised she was better at shopping for clothes than making them. The next morning, Thea scampered into the kitchen. In one paw she held a cup of steaming coffee. In the other was a wad of papers. **"HERE IT IS!"** she announced. "The answer to our guidebook problem!"

I chewed my whiskers nervously. What had Thea cooked up this time? There was no way she'd get me in a dress again. And I put my paw down at the thought of **HIGH HEELS**.

"Don't look so worried, **Gerry Berry**," my sister giggled. "My idea is really very simple."

And it was. No mouse would want to buy a guidebook on Ratzikistan, Thea reminded us. But every mouse would love to sink his or her teeth into some delicious Cheddarella cheese.

"Instead of a guidebook, we'll publish a cookbook!"

Thea squeaked. **"We can fill it with yummy Cheddarella cheese recipes!"**

OUR COSY HOME

We had all kinds of adventures on our way home.

One day, we got stuck in the middle of the woods. A tree had fallen in front of our camper van. To get through, we had to saw it into small pieces. Can you guess who did all of the sawing? You guessed it! **I HAD BLISTERS ALL OVER MY PAWS!**

After that, we had a flat tyre. We were trying to avoid a caribou.

Later on, we got caught in a **SNOWSTORM**. We were snowed in for three days.

Tina kept our spirits up with her delicious **CHEDDARELLA** cheese dishes. Plus, I must admit it was nice to be together. **I was getting used to our cosy four-wheeled home.**

ONE THING AT A TIME

I sat next to Grandfather on the way home. I had to give it to the old mouse. He never seemed to get tired. He was stuck to the wheel from dawn till dusk. He never spoke while driving. "When I am driving, I concentrate on the road," he explained. "The secret of success, **GEROMINO**, is to do just one thing at a time!"

I thought about what Grandfather had said. I watched the road unfolding before us. It was pretty fascinating. At each turn, we saw something different.

Maybe travelling wasn't so bad after all, I decided. Still, I couldn't wait to get back to my **comfy mouse hole**. I'd slip my paws into My cat-fur slippers. I'd whip up a tasty mozzarella milkshake. I mean, don't get me wrong, Grandfather William's super camper van was awesome. But I love my home sweet home.

"You look tired, **GERONIMO**," Grandfather observed. "Why don't you get some rest? I'll be fine."

I smiled. Yes, Grandfather could be obnoxious at times. He was one rodent who really knew how to drive me up a clock. But he really wasn't such a bad mouse.

He had lots of **crazy ideas**, sure, but some of them were good ones.

And I knew that no matter what, he loved me.

ANOTHER DAY, ANOTHER ADVENTURE

When I woke up, I spotted a sign on the side of the road. **CHEESE NIBLETS!** We were almost home!

Welcome to NEW MOUSE CITY

Grandfather let me drive the rest of the way. Of course, he had to scream a few commands from the back seat. "**NOT TOO FAST! NOT TOO SLOW! STOP ON RED! GO ON GREEN!**" he called.

I didn't even care. We were going home.

At last, we reached New Mouse City. Rodents rushed along the sidewalks.

Taxis SCREECHED and honked their horns. Buildings touched the sky. Ah, beautiful New Mouse

City. Have you ever been there? There's really no place like it!

Even though I was thrilled to be home, I felt sad leaving everyone. I was used to Tina's **yummy meals**. (Although I could do without the force-feeding.) And Grandfather had grown on me.

"The best way to get to know a rodent is to travel with him," Grandfather always said. I guess he was right. I knew a lot about Grandfather after this trip.

I climbed out in front of my house. Thea called a taxi. Grandfather William and Tina boarded the camper van again.

"Will I see you tomorrow, Grandfather?" I asked.

He chuckled. "Who knows, **GERONIMO?**" he

replied. "Tomorrow is another day. Another day, another **ADVENTURE!**"

Tina waved goodbye with her silver rolling pin. **Then they both vanished into the night.**

JUST GRANDFATHER

Would you like to know how it all ended? Well, let me tell you. Our cookbook, **'SECRET RECIPES FROM RATZIKISTAN'**, was a huge success.

Three million copies were sold! Yesterday I got an email from Grandfather. *"SEE? I TOLD YOU SO! THREE MILLION COPIES! THREE! THREE!!!"* he wrote.

Did I mention that Grandfather **loves** it when he's right?

I have stopped saying that I hate travelling. I mean, how else can you see the world? I am even planning a **Christmas** trip with the family!

Yes, Thea and Trap will pick on me. Tina will make me eat tonnes of food.

And Grandfather, well, he'll just be Grandfather.

But I guess that's not such a bad thing after all ...

ABOUT THE AUTHOR

Born in New Mouse City, Mouse Island, GERONIMO STILTON is Rattus Emeritus of Mousomorphic Literature and of Neo-Ratonic Comparative Philosophy. For the past twenty years, he has been running The Rodent's Gazette, New Mouse City's most widely read daily newspaper.

Stilton was awarded the Ratitzer Prize for his scoops on *The Curse of the Cheese Pyramid* and *The Search for Sunken Treasure*. He has also received the Andersen Prize

for Personality of the Year. His works have been published all over the globe.

In his spare time, Mr. Stilton collects antique cheese rinds and plays golf. But what he most enjoys is telling stories to his nephew Benjamin.

THE RODENT'S GAZETTE

1. Main entrance
2. Printing presses (where everything is printed)
3. Accounts department
4. Editorial room (where editors, illustrators, and designers work)
5. Geronimo Stilton's office
6. Geronimo's botanical garden

MAP OF NEW MOUSE CITY

MAP OF MOUSE ISLAND

1. Big Ice Lake
2. Frozen Fur Peak
3. Slipperyslopes Glacier
4. Coldcreeps Peak
5. Ratzikistan
6. Transratania
7. Mount Vamp
8. Roastedrat Volcano
9. Brimstone Lake
10. Poopedcat Pass
11. Stinko Peak
12. Dark Forest
13. Vain Vampires Valley
14. Goosebumps Gorge
15. The Shadow Line Pass
16. Penny-Pincher Castle
17. Nature Reserve Park
18. Las Ratayas Marinas
19. Fossil Forest
20. Lake Lake
21. Lake Lakelake
22. Lake Lakelakelake
23. Cheddar Crag

24. Cannycat Castle
25. Valley of the Giant Sequoia
26. Cheddar Springs
27. Sulphurous Swamp
28. Old Reliable Geyser
29. Vole Vale
30. Ravingrat Ravine
31. Gnat Marshes
32. Munster Highlands
33. Mousehara Desert
34. Oasis of the Sweaty Camel
35. Cabbagehead Hill
36. Rattytrap Jungle
37. Rio Mosquito
38. Mousefort Beach
39. San Mouscisco
40. Swissville
41. Cheddarton
42. Mouseport
43. New Mouse City
44. Pirate Ship of Cats

THE COLLECTION

HAVE YOU READ ALL OF GERONIMO'S ADVENTURES?

☐ *Lost Treasure of the Emerald Eye*

☐ *The Curse of the Cheese Pyramid*

☐ *Cat and Mouse in a Haunted House*

☐ *I'm Too Fond of My Fur!*

☐ *Four Mice Deep in the Jungle*

☐ *Paws Off, Cheddarface!*

☐ *Fangs and Feasts in Transratania*

☐ *Attack of the Pirate Cats*

HAPPY READING!